Mighty Stallion 2

Fury's Journey

Follow in the hoof prints of Sariavo's stepson, Fury…

………..Keeping up with the responsibilities of being the next Mighty Stallion wasn't as easy as Fury had thought. With the privilege came the duty to see his father's honor upheld…and Fury's journey to find his own courage. ……

Mighty Stallion 2

Fury's Journey

The Sequel to Mighty Stallion

By: Victoria Kasten

Original cover by James Krom Natural Images

Second Printing • 750 copies • March 2007

Library of Congress Control Number: 2005909573
ISBN: 978-0-9788850-1-4

Additional copies of this book are available by mail. See back
pages for information. Send comments/payments to:

Mighty Stallion Books
5465 Glencoe Ave
Webster, MN 55088

Published By: Victoria Kasten

Printed in the USA by
Morris Publishing
3212 East Highway 30
Kearney, NE 68847
1-800-650-7888

To: Uncle Jim

Thank you so much for your beautiful artwork.
The covers of these books are a great tribute to
your amazing talent.

TABLE OF CONTENTS

~ 1 ~

A New Journey Begins

Sariavo stood on the hill overlooking the cave, and took a deep breath as he surveyed his surroundings. The fall aromas filled his nostrils. There were the scents of the leaves that lay all over the ground, and the scents of the autumn air, its chill becoming slightly noticeable.

He watched the clear waterfall cascade down and tumble into a pool beside the entrance of the cave. White water lilies floated silently in the cool water. Soft green moss grew over the rocks at the edge of the pool adding a splash of color to the gray stone. "It feels so good to be home," Sariavo thought to himself.

Sariavo had returned to his home three months ago. With him had come Penny, and Fury. The rest of the herd he had taken from Thunderbird had not been eager to join a new larger herd, so Sariavo had sent them off with a young stallion at their head. Only Penny and Fury had stayed behind with him.

Coming home had been one of the most joyful times of Sariavo's life. He had been afraid that he would never see his parents or Sari again. They had been very surprised and happy to see him when he had returned.

After his parents and their herd had greeted him, Sariavo had told them all about his adventures, whom he'd met and what he'd seen. They had listened with vast interest, and had congratulated him on his accomplishments.

After the initial excitement, Sariavo had discovered that Sari had a surprise of her own. Sari had been pregnant with his foal when Sariavo disappeared, but she had not known.

Now, eleven months after he'd been captured, Sari had given him Novana, a small black filly who was her mother's image. Sariavo was very proud of her. She was the cutest foal for miles around.

Novana was a deep black in color, with a white star, and two white socks on her hind legs. Her head was the image of her mother's. Long lashes shadowed her dark eyes, her nose dipped in a slight dish face, and her fluted nostrils bespoke of her Arabian heritage from her mother. Her slender legs were delicate and fine boned. Her shoulders were narrow but powerful.

Novana's mother, Sari, was half Arabian and half Andalusian, and she had passed on the best of both breeds to her beautiful new daughter.

Sariavo was also very proud of his adopted son Fury. Fury was Novana's older stepbrother by three months and was now five and a half months old.

At first Fury wasn't sure about sharing Sariavo because he had liked the sole attention of his stepfather and hero. Soon though, Fury began to accept Novana as part of his new family. He began bringing her little gifts, like leaves and twigs.

Sariavo smiled to himself as he thought about his family. He was pleased that he had a herd of his own. Sariavo felt blessed that all those that he loved once again surrounded him. With that last thought he trotted back down the hill.

******

Sari and Penny had been watching their foals too. The two mothers had strong hopes that Novana and Fury would one day be more than just playmates.

****

Fury and Novana were soon each other's best friends. They loved to go on little "adventures" through the woods and meadows. They were allowed to go wherever they pleased, because unknown to them, out of sight, Sariavo was always following and making sure they were out of trouble.

One of the foals' favorite places was a large meadow with grass that grew up to their shoulders. There were many kinds of wildflowers that grew in that meadow and Novana liked to lie in the long grass and smell them. Fury did this with her sometimes, but smelling flowers wasn't his idea of an adventure. So he would race around the meadow as fast as he could, every day trying to go faster and faster. He wanted to be as fast as Sariavo when he was older.

The foals also spent hours every day pretending that they were on great adventures. Fury couldn't wait until he was old enough to really go exploring. There was so much he wanted to see and do.

While Novana smelled flowers and Fury raced, Sariavo would watch over his two foals with grave severity. He was always on watch for the predators of the wild. A wild cougar would eagerly chase after a young colt or filly if he knew that the foal was alone. So Sariavo was ever watchful for the dangers that lurked, unknown to either of the foals.

~ 2 ~

A Good Father

Sariavo was relaxing in the pool that was in his cave room. The warm water lapped around his shoulders, easing away the aches of the day's events. As he lay in the pool, he thought about his newest surprises. Both of his mares were in foal.

A few months after his return home, Penny had announced that she was pregnant with her second foal. Penny was very anxious for its arrival, as this time the foal was Sariavo's.

Sari had been happy for her friend, but her joy became even more complete when she found out that she too, was in foal. Sari was so happy to give Sariavo another foal.

With two new foals on the way, Sariavo was kept busier than ever accommodating the needs of his two mares plus his daughter and stepson.

Sariavo's thoughts were interrupted as he heard a quiet step at the door. Fury's little red head appeared.

"Hello, Sariavo!" he said cheerfully, and walked over to the pool's edge. Sariavo nuzzled the colt's stubbly mane affectionately.

"Hello, Fury. What do you need?" the stallion asked. Fury frowned.

"When will Mother's foal get here? It's taking an awfully long time," the colt commented quietly. Sariavo smiled.

"Foals do take a long time. But it will be here soon." Fury looked thoughtful.

"I hope it's a boy, like me. I want a little brother," the colt said. Sariavo laughed.

"That would be nice. But we'll like whatever your mother gives us, won't we?" Sariavo said with a serious look at his stepson. The colt smiled brightly.

"Yup! We will."

Suddenly, Novana came trotting into the room.

"Hi, Daddy!" she exclaimed brightly. Sariavo nuzzled her.

"Hello, sweetness." Novana giggled as Sariavo's tongue tickled her face. Soon, the foals were engaging in some good-natured teasing with each other behind Sariavo, but he paid no attention to it.

Sariavo finally got out of the water and shook himself dry. He went out of his room, with the two foals dogging his heels.

Sariavo stopped at the room of his favorite mare, Sari, and shooed the foals out. They went trotting outside to play.

Sari looked up at Sariavo from her leafy bed. Sariavo smiled at her.

"How are you?" he asked. Sari tossed her mane.

"I'm fine. Just fine," she answered quietly. She slowly stood up, being careful not to jostle the foal. Sariavo reached out and bumped her belly with his nose. Nothing happened. Sariavo sighed.

"I guess he's not big enough to play yet," he teased Sari. She shook her head in amusement.

"Sariavo, *she* is barely a few weeks old. She's about half the size of one of your teeth."

Sariavo sighed. "I wish he would hurry up and come out." Sari laughed.

"Now you sound like Fury," she told him. The cave was filled with the sound of their laughter.

******

One year later, both foals had been born. Sari had presented Sariavo with his second daughter, named Saria. This filly was a chocolate brown color, and she looked more like Sariavo. Her bone structure was heavier than Novana's.

Penny's foal was a bright chestnut colt that they named Prince. The little colt was a joy to the whole family, for he was a very happy foal. He never got angry with his siblings or parents, and was content to simply lay in the sunshine and sleep.

****

Sariavo laughed as his newest daughter, Saria, played with his tail. She was pulling on it with her tiny yellow teeth. Novana and Fury were out in the meadow, chasing each other in circles. Sariavo noticed that they suddenly stopped and began talking in raised voices.

"Father likes me best!" Novana hissed at Fury.

"No he doesn't! I'm his favorite, because I'm a boy. You're just a good for nothing girl," Fury informed Novana.

"Well! So that's how you talk to a lady? Shame on you."

Fury grinned, "Yup, and ladies are sweet and beautiful, which you are not, so I guess you aren't a lady."

Novana gasped. "I'm telling Mother!" She turned and ran right into her father. Sariavo stopped her.

"What seems to be the problem, Novana? I heard yelling."

Novana hung her head. "He says I'm a good-for-nothing girl, Daddy, and he says that you like him best." Sariavo's eyes started dancing with amusement.

"He does, does he? Well, we can't have that, can we?" Novana shook her head vigorously. Sariavo suddenly lunged forward, and tackled Fury, pushing the young colt over with his nose. Fury squealed and kicked.

"Sariavo! Don't do that!" But he erupted into giggles, for his father was tickling him. Novana squealed with delight.

"Get him, Daddy! Get him!" Sariavo then gently pushed Novana on top of Fury, and tickled them both with the black whiskers on his muzzle. By the time they were done, both Fury and Novana had forgotten all about their fight.

~ 3 ~

Fury's Honor

By his second birthday, Fury was almost as big as Sariavo, and he never let anyone forget that he was almost a stallion. His father always said that he was going to be a very good herd leader someday.

Novana was different too. Her ebony black coat shone and shimmered. Her long mane reached down to her shoulder, and her tail to her ankles. She still did tease Fury about being "an awfully boastful stallion". That always made him grin.

Sariavo, Sari and Penny had decided to ask the two young horses about being mates. Sariavo asked Fury and Novana to take a walk with him in the woods.

They obliged willingly, but curiously. As they walked, Sariavo turned his head to look back at the two young horses.

"Fury, Novana, your mothers and I were wondering if the two of you were interested in starting a herd of your own. I was wondering also, Novana, if you are interested in becoming Fury's mate."

Fury and Novana both stared at their father. Fury felt very awkward. Novana had expected this to come, but she hadn't been entirely prepared for it. She sighed.

"Well…I suppose. I guess I wouldn't mind it."

But Sariavo wasn't satisfied. "Novana, I don't want you to say yes because it's what I want. If you love Fury, then say yes. But not otherwise."

Fury stepped in calmly. "Can we talk about it for a day or two, Sariavo?" he asked.

Sariavo smiled. "That would be fine. We're in no hurry."

Fury thanked him, and Sariavo left to go back to the cave. Novana stood overlooking the meadow where they had played as foals. Her black mane whipped back in the cool wind. Fury felt a lump rising in his throat.

Suddenly, he felt very uncomfortable. He turned away and watched a squirrel running up a tree.

He heard a soft voice behind him.

"Fury?"

It was Novana. Fury turned around slowly, and faced her. He opened his mouth, but quickly shut it. Novana smiled.

"I think I've made a decision," she told him. Fury was surprised.

"So soon? But Father said we could have a day or two to talk it over."

Novana shook her head. "No. I would love to be a part of your herd if you'll have me."

Fury let out a deep breath of relief. "Thank you, Novana. I will be honored."

Novana laughed. "Don't be silly, Fury. There are thousands of pretty mares out there. You don't have to choose me."

Fury nodded. "Yes I do. Because I love you."

Novana looked up at him in surprise. "Really?" she asked, as if unbelieving.

Fury nodded again to confirm it. "Yes, really."

Novana suddenly touched her nose to Fury's. Fury's eyes flew open wide in surprise, and then he stood staring as Novana drew back and turned around. She raced through the trees and disappeared.

It was a fully five minutes before Fury could move.

"Wow…. she loves me," he said excitedly. He tossed his mane and bellowed, and then ran after Novana towards the cave.

******

Novana and Fury were looking forward to starting a herd of their own. Their parents had been very excited to learn that the two of them were in love. Fury had talked Sariavo into letting them go on a long trip somewhere farther west. Fury said he wanted to find a place to start his own herd, which might have been part of his intent, but the real reason was that he wanted to be alone with Novana. Of course, he also wanted to prove that he was as powerful as any other stallion for miles around.

But all their hopes were put on hold when little Prince suddenly became very sick. The chestnut colt complained of a very sore stomach, and Penny was watching over him constantly.

One night, soon after Sariavo and his family had dropped off to sleep, Prince was violently ill from colic. Penny helped him to get up and kept him walking around, but by midnight, Prince was gone.

Penny tearfully woke the other family members and told them that their little Prince was dead.

When Sariavo heard, he closed his eyes and his head hung low with grief. He wanted to go off and be by himself, but he stayed because Penny needed him. He slept in her room that night, trying his best to comfort the distraught mare. She cried for hours.

She finally fell into a fitful sleep just when the barest of light was beginning to shine over the mountains.

~ 4 ~

New Beginnings

When Sariavo left Penny, he went outside to find Fury. The young chestnut stallion was standing in the meadow. Sariavo walked over to stand beside his stepson.

"Fury, I want you and Novana to go. Begin your journey."

Fury stared at the older stallion. "But Mother needs me right now. She just lost her foal…and he was your son."

Sariavo looked at Fury closely. He noticed the sadness in the dark eyes of his stepson.

"What do you mean by that, Fury?" asked Sariavo gravely. The younger stallion huffed and turned away.

"She was so proud of him. She finally had her dream son. He was yours, and hers. What she wanted from the day she met you."

Sariavo frowned. "Fury, just because I did not sire you does not mean you are not my son. I have always loved you as if you were. So why the jealousy now?"

Fury shrugged as if it didn't matter. But Sariavo was patient.

He waited until Fury finally said, "Because I wish that I was your real son."

Sariavo sighed. "Loyalty is not measured by heritage, Fury. Your real father was a scoundrel. But you have two parents, and your other parent is Penny. You are a lot like her. You are a true Mighty Stallion spirit. Your heritage from her formed you into who you are. And even if you were my real son, I couldn't be any prouder of you than I am now."

Fury smiled a little. "Really?" Sariavo nodded.

"Really. Now you and Novana go have an adventure. I want to hear all about it when you come back."

Fury reared in excitement and galloped to the cave to tell Novana to get ready. Sariavo watched him with a wistful eye. He knew that many questions were still waiting to be answered. Someday, maybe, he would tell Fury about his real father. But for now, Sariavo was content to let it lie.

******

The very next morning, Fury and Novana started out. Novana seemed as eager to go as Fury. They kept up a brisk trot for an hour or so, and then Novana stopped to get a drink.

"I'm just going to see what is on the other side of this hill," Fury told her. He looked over the other side to see a small herd of elk feeding. That instantly made him cautious. Mountain lions love elk meat, so where there was an elk herd, there was almost certain to be at least one cougar trailing it. Fury turned to go back and tell Novana what he had seen; when from that direction he heard a cat screech, and "Fury! Help!" from Novana!

He whirled and charged back. His racing legs pounded rhythmically on the grassy plain.

He came into the small clearing. There was Novana, bucking and rearing, with a cougar clinging to her back. When Fury came racing back, he crashed into the young mare with so much force it threw her off the ground, pinning the cat beneath her. The combined weight of the two horses didn't give the cougar a chance. Novana felt the claws slowly fall away.

When Fury let her up, Novana shuddered. "Thanks." She smiled up at him, and Fury's heart melted.

"It was nothing," he answered quietly. After cleaning Novana's cuts in a river, they continued on their way.

They changed course and left the forest they had been traveling through. They struck out across a wide-open prairie land that had knee high grasses waving as far as their eyes could see. Fury eagerly anticipated finding a herd soon, because the country they were traveling in was prime grazing land.

******

Fall came, dispatching thousands of leaves from many different trees. Novana was acting strangely. No longer did she wish to join Fury in his wild races around a meadow. No longer did she wish to dance and play. She ran only when pursued, and then it wasn't very fast. Fury also noticed that her usually slim barrel (middle) was growing round and fat. He didn't say anything, because he wasn't sure he should.

Novana wanted to rest and drink more and more. Fury was starting to get restless. He wanted to race and run, to give play to his powerful muscles. But he also wanted a horse to do it with. Novana couldn't, and none of the forest and meadow animals were friendly. He began to get lonely.

~ 5 ~

Parents To Be

On a cool fall night, several days later, Novana finally decided to tell Fury what was 'wrong'. She found him looking up at the stars, talking to himself.

"Fury, I want to tell you something." Fury turned to her, and grinned.

"Bout time," he said.

"I'm in foal to you," Novana hung her head, but jerked it up when she heard a chuckle.

"I thought that might be what was causing this small change," Fury said, nudging Novana's extra large belly. She laughed merrily. The exciting promise of a new baby kept both the anxious parents up talking for half the night. But when they finally did fall asleep, Fury and Novana slept better than they had in days.

******

The two horses spent their time alone in the forested hills for the next few months. They played some, but Novana still didn't want to do anything too hard. Fury began to get extremely restless. He would go off on his own now and then, and try to locate a friendly herd. But he had no luck. There was no herd for miles. Finally, he persuaded Novana to move with him farther west.

It was a long week that they traveled. They kept on for hours on end, only stopping for quick drinks or an hour's rest.

Then, one day, the pair of weary travelers came into sight of a horse herd grazing peacefully in a large clearing. Novana laughed for joy at the sight of other horses, and then started towards them. Fury stopped her.

"Why, Fury, what is it?" she wanted to know. Fury looked towards the woods.

"I just want to make sure it's safe before we meet the herd."

Fury trotted toward the trees and disappeared. Novana grew impatient waiting and decided to take another look at the other horses. She cantered toward the ridge overlooking the herd and closely studied each of the mares.

She also saw a handsome sorrel stallion emerge from the herd. The stallion was very muscular and powerful. His shoulders were heavy and broad. His head was only slightly bigger than Fury's. But he wasn't purebred, Novana could tell.

He surveyed his surroundings and fixed his black eyes fiercely on Novana. He started when he saw her.

Here was a beautiful black mare that he could add to his harem.

The big sorrel cantered up to Novana making soft noises to her in his throat. Novana laced her ears back and pawed the ground. The stallion stopped about three yards away from her.

"I'm Samson", he said gently. Novana snorted warily.

"I'm Novana. I'm from Sariavo's herd. I'm not interested in joining your herd. Leave me alone," she said, pinning her ears back even tighter. Her lips lifted slightly, revealing her teeth. She looked anything but friendly.

Samson's eyes narrowed in sudden discomfort, for Sariavo's name was well known for miles. And Samson had no intentions of angering the powerful stallion. But he looked around carefully, and saw no other horses.

"Are you alone?" he asked her in an ominous voice. Novana looked up at him, her dark eyes flashing in anger.

"I can take care of myself, thank you," she said, quickly glancing in Fury's direction. She was getting worried that he hadn't made an appearance yet. She turned back to Samson.

"You're wasting your time. I am not interested in being a broodmare. I'm on a journey to see more of the country, and you're not going to stop me."

Samson laughed. "You might change your mind. I am very powerful, you know. I'm feared for miles around. Besides," he said, glancing amusedly at her belly, "It looks like you're already planning on a family".

Novana kicked at him with her front legs. "That is none of your business, so leave me alone, and go away. I am not going to come with you." Novana turned to leave, but Samson was faster, and he stepped in front of her.

"Yes you are." he said, no longer friendly. He wanted Novana, and would stop at nothing to get her. He bit her roughly on her flank, and she screamed and tried to rear, but the extra weight of the foal was too much. She tried to run, but Samson jostled her so hard, that she fell heavily on her side, groaning.

Just then, Fury appeared. He charged from the trees with the anger and fierceness of a hurricane, and crashed his big body into the startled Samson. The herd had by now noticed what was going on, and cheered Fury on, because they didn't like Samson. He was too rough and mean to them. Fury threw Samson to the ground and stood over him, his lips drawn back to expose white teeth.

"This is what happens when you rough up my girl," Fury hissed. His hooves lifted slightly over Samson's shoulders. Samson's eyes closed as he braced himself. But the blow never fell.

Opening his eyes, Samson saw Fury attending to Novana. Samson stared at him.

"Why didn't you kill me?" he asked in amazement. Fury looked back at him.

"The horses that begin as enemies sometimes play a part in the shaping of what you become. I'm not interested in having your blood on my name."

Samson's eyes filled with admiration, but he said nothing for several minutes. Then, he got to his feet and took off, running away as fast as he could. Fury turned to Novana, who was still lying on the grass, puffing.

Fury spoke softly to her. "Forgive me, Novana. I shouldn't have gone into the forest and left you."

Novana sighed and closed her eyes. "I'm...fine. I think. It's not your fault, Fury."

Suddenly, from the middle of the herd, a big mare that was missing an eye stepped forward.

"Welcome, stallion. You are very welcome here. Samson was a terrible leader."

Fury smiled. "Thank you, but I have to confess, I have no experience in taking care of a herd."

The big mare tossed her short mane. "We will help you. Don't worry about a thing. I'm Diamond, the lead mare of this herd."

She showed him his new family, and Fury discovered that his herd consisted of fourteen mares and two geldings, who helped watch out for the mares. The geldings, Jake and Runner, had escaped from humans a few years back.

Diamond was the lead mare, like she had told Fury, which meant that she took care of the herd when the stallion wasn't around.

Fury went back to Novana, and looked down at her concernedly when he saw she was still lying down.

"Novana? Are you okay?" he asked. She smiled and nodded.

"I'm fine," she answered. She stuck her legs out in front of her and hoisted herself up. But she huffed when she got up, and quickly lay back down. Fury was now extremely concerned.

"What's wrong, Novana?" he wanted to know. She tossed her mane, and looking up at him, "I think your foal decided it's not going to wait any longer. Go, I'll be fine."

Fury's eyes had widened. He was filled with a mix of emotions: excitement, happiness, and worry. But he honored her wishes. After nuzzling Novana's face encouragingly, he went for a walk in the woods and left her with Diamond.

******

An hour later, when Fury returned, a skinny, pure white foal was nursing at Novana's side. Fury was filled with pride as he stepped from the woods to see his new son. He flew towards the exhausted mare and her foal. Novana looked up at him when he came.

"Do you like him?" she asked, excitement filling her large black eyes. Fury nuzzled the sleepy colt.

"Yes, he is beautiful. Thank you, Novana."

Novana licked the colt as he fell asleep at her feet.

"What shall we call him?" she asked. "I can't think of anything."

Fury studied every feature of the colt. He had Novana's gentle eyes, but everything else was the image of his father. Fury smiled as the colt started to snore softly.

"Let's call him Glory."

Novana sighed wearily. "Glory…that is a good name. A strong name for the son of Fury." She smiled up at her mate, and beamed when she saw the love reflecting in his eyes.

~ 6 ~

The Love of a Mother

Little Glory was a joy to the whole herd. He kept them all busy answering his many questions. The colt was so full of life and excitement. Everything was an adventure to him.

Fury was very proud of his son. Glory was a fine addition to the famous bloodline of Regal and Sariavo.

But Novana was the proudest of all. Her love for her son was overpowering. She scarcely let him out of her sight. But he knew that his mother was very concerned for him, and so he didn't mind. Glory loved it when his father played with him. Fury would race him around the meadow, letting Glory try out his galloping, which was getting smoother and faster every day.

One day, Fury and Novana were leading their herd toward Sariavo's cave. Glory had trotted off into the trees on the left side of the herd's path.

Suddenly, the herd was aware of a bone chilling sound. It was the frantic whinny of a colt. Fury whirled, looking for the owner of the voice. What he heard next made his blood chill.

"Father! Help, a wolf!" It was Glory. Terrified for his son, Fury raced towards the frightening sound. When he got there, he saw Glory running towards him as fast as his small legs could go. Behind him, closing in fast, came a huge lobo buffalo wolf, white fangs ready to slash the tendons in Glory's legs.

Fury was so intent on reaching Glory that he did not see two other things. One was the rest of the wolf pack, about ten of them, running hard to help their friend make the kill.

The other was Novana, who was closer to the wolf pack than Fury. She was pumping her legs as hard as she could, racing straight towards the ground in front of the wolves. She got there before Fury, and threw herself between the pack and her son.

Fury, meanwhile, was dealing with the wolf that had been chasing Glory. The big red stallion had put an end to that lobo right away. Then he saw Novana, trying to keep all the other wolves away from Glory. She was lathered in sweat and bleeding profusely. Novana was exhausted, and the wolves were ready to kill her.

Fury furiously charged right into the middle of the pack, bellowing angrily. After a few vain attempts to bring the big red stallion down, the wolves ran off in search of easier game. Novana tried to remain standing, but collapsed in a heap at Fury's feet.

She huffed, and the cold November breeze froze her breath in midair. Glory came up, still shaking from the shock of everything, and glanced anxiously at his mother.

"Dad? What's wrong with Mother?" The little colt looked up at his father.

"She…she…" Fury couldn't finish. Novana lifted her eyes, and smiled weakly at the two concerned males.

"Fury…Fury, listen to me. I don't know if I'm going to make it to Sariavo's cave. Take Glory along, and keep going west, or return to your father's herd. Leave me here, I'll manage." But Fury shook his beautifully sculpted head vigorously.

"No! The wolves…they'll come back, and you are in no condition to fight them again. They'll kill you for sure." Novana nodded.

"Maybe you're right. But you and Fury go on. I'll come later, when I'm feeling better." Still, Fury refused.

"Novana, I can't just leave you here. I won't let you die."

The herd rushed up, huffing and breathing. They had been delayed by the retreating wolf pack when they had vainly attempted to follow the flying red stallion.

Novana was helped up by two geldings, which stood on either side of her to support her as she walked. Novana held her head up, with all the dignity of a queen. The two geldings, Jake and Runner, were very good at doctoring wounded horses, so they took Novana off a little ways and began cleaning the bites on her legs. Fury soon learned that though the wounds were painful for his mare, she would recover.

Fury looked at Glory. The colt was prancing around in circles. Now that both Novana and Glory were safe and sound, Fury felt an overpowering urge to race and run. He turned to his son.

"Glory, want to race?' Fury asked.

Glory nodded eagerly, and the two ran off in a mad chase through the woods. Novana watched them, and smiled.

"I believe Fury will be happy to know that I am again in foal to him." The herd exchanged grins, and soft murmurs of approval were heard. Diamond walked up to the black mare.

"Yes, you are right. He will be very proud." Fury raced up.

"I will be proud of what?" Novana laughed, in her happy, loving voice.

"You are going to be a father again, Fury." Fury bellowed happily, the sound echoing through the canyon walls.

~ 7 ~

Fury's Second Foal

Once Novana was well enough to travel, Fury and his herd began to slowly make their way back towards the cave and Sariavo's family. It was a long trip back, but Fury was looking forward to seeing his father and mother again. Novana too, was eager to return to her home. Glory was excited to meet his grandfather, of whom his father had told him many great tales.

******

Spring came, bringing with it sounds that were a joy to the weary travelers. A small chestnut mare named Echo announced softly that she was going to have Fury's foal too. But even though the herd welcomed the thought of the more powerful bloodline addition to their herd, Fury still only loved Novana. She alone held his heart.

Over the next three months, her belly swelled to a great size. Fury one day boldly examined her, and announced that she would have a colt. Novana laughed.

"Oh, Fury! It's too early to tell!" But she too hoped for a colt.

******

Glory was growing like a weed, and he now stood only a few inches below Novana. He was proud that he was almost up to Fury's shoulder, and still growing. Fury expected his son to pass him in height. Glory boasted to everyone that he would beat up every other stallion in the world. Fury chuckled.

"My son is everything he should be…except humble." Novana just shook her head. " That boy," she would say.

All the herd members loved Glory, especially Diamond. She cooed over him, babied him, and spoiled him. Glory pulled beautiful meadow wildflowers with his big yellow teeth, and brought them to her every day, for there were plenty of the flowered plants.

Fury estimated that they were about 50 or so miles away from Sariavo and his herd. It was July now, and Fury made plans to return to Sariavo's herd soon after Novana's foal came.

Glory was eager to meet his grandfather, because Fury had told him all about Sariavo's journey. Glory told everyone that Sariavo was his hero. Fury grinned, remembering how he had idolized his father when he was young.

******

In the first week of August, Novana gave birth to a chestnut filly. Fury proudly named her Inahu, which meant: 'beautiful'. She was very slender, like her mother, and had Novana's general features. The whole herd was extremely proud of her, because she was only a few days old, and already she showed that she would be a gorgeous mare when she grew up.

Glory, however, was not excited about the arrival of his sister. He took his problem to Fury.

"Dad, uh, can I talk to you?" he asked on day. Fury smiled.

"Sure, what's on your mind?" Glory hung his head.

"Will you race around the meadow with me?" Fury shook his head.

"I would love to, Glory," Fury began. "But I'm helping your mother with Inahu."

Angrily, Glory's head shot up. "That is what you always say. That's what everybody says. Nobody cares about boring old me anymore; they're all too busy with *the princess Inahu*."

Glory spit the name out, as if it were a nasty taste on his tongue. Before Fury had a chance to respond,

- 33 -

Glory whirled away and raced off in the direction of the woods. Fury didn't follow, because he knew his son just needed to be by himself.

~ 8 ~

Glory In Danger

Later that evening, just as Fury was dozing off, Novana appeared by his side. Fury woke and looked at her questioningly.

Novana hushed him, "Shh. Don't wake the others. I'm very worried, because Glory hasn't come back yet."

After Novana's words sank in, Fury immediately set off in the direction the colt had taken. Before long, he saw the body of a white colt in the distance. Fury cried out, and flew towards the young horse.

"Glory! Glory, talk to me!" he said. But Glory's eyes didn't open. Fury burrowed his nose under the colt's shoulders, and grunted as he slid his son's body to his back. He wobbled a little under the weight of the colt, but he determinedly began walking slowly back to the herd. After an agonizing hour, the red stallion came in sight of the herd.

Novana screamed when she saw the limp body of her son across Fury's shoulders.

"I think he tangled with another stallion," Fury said. Novana sobbed and tears rolled down her cheeks. Fury spoke.

"Novana, he is alive, but if I do not get him to my father soon…" he didn't need to say anything else. Novana was hurrying him off.

******

Fury arrived at the old herd before night fell. His mother hurried over, and gasped when she saw Glory. After nuzzling Fury in greeting, she asked, "Who is that, Fury?"

Fury looked into her worried eyes. "He is my son."

Penny looked from Fury to Glory, then back to Fury.

"With Novana?" she questioned. Fury nodded.

"He is hurt. Where is my father?"

Penny gestured toward the cave. "He is swimming with Sari."

Fury entered the cave, and saw his father and Sari, swimming around the big pool in the front of the cave, pushing each other under the water. Sariavo glanced up and saw Fury, and climbed out of the pool. Water streamed from his mane and tail. Sari stared at the white colt on Fury's back before gracefully stepping out of the water.

"Your son?"

Fury proudly nodded. "Yes, but he's hurt. I was hoping you could help."

Sariavo took the colt from Fury, and then disappeared into his own bedchamber. Sari gracefully stepped out of the pool, and looked in the direction that Sariavo had gone. "You and Novana did well. He is a fine colt." Fury beamed.

"We are proud of him. We also have a daughter, named Inahu." Sari smiled.

"That was my mother's name."

Fury grinned. "It means 'beautiful', and she certainly is all that and more."

~ 9 ~

Fury's Return

Glory's strength returned very slowly. Fury was worried that his son would not regain the use of his front legs. Sariavo, however, did not share that opinion.

"Glory is from a line of magnificent stallions," he said. "That colt has a lot in his favor."

Sari and Penny were doting grandmothers. They played games like race from the humans and tag with Glory, to strengthen his legs and muscles. But Fury grew restless. He wanted to go back to Novana, but Glory was having such a good time that Fury was reluctant to go.

******

The next day, Fury called Glory to him.

"Yes, Dad?" the colt was out of breath from running with Penny.

"Glory, how would you like to stay with Grandma and Grandpa, and Grandma Penny while I go get your mother and the other horses?" Glory's eyes grew excited.

"Oh, can I?" Fury smiled at his son.

"Sure. I asked your grandparents if they would be okay with that. And they said yes. I'll see you in a week or so."

Glory ran to Grandpa Sariavo, yelling, "I get to stay with you!" Fury grinned again, and streaked off into the woods.

The day after leaving his son, Fury found the valley that he'd left Novana and the others. He thundered over the hill, screaming a greeting. He waited. Silence.

Curiously, he looked over the cliff wall. The valley was empty. Fury felt panic rising in his throat. Where was his herd? Then he heard angry whistles in the distance, followed by a frightened whinny. It was Novana.

Fury took off in the direction of his mare's voice, which was somewhere between frightened and pure rage. When he got very close, Fury silently moved slowly toward his destination. Then he saw his herd.

His sleek and beautiful herd was mixed in with a bunch of shaggy, heavily pregnant mares. Novana was lying on the ground, her sides and neck covered with patches of sweat. A stallion, bigger than Fury, was standing next to her, a triumphant smile on his face.

"Forget your stinking stallion! You're MINE!" The stallion cried, pure glee in his voice. Fury's ears laced back so tight to his head that his head hurt. His lips rose, exposing two rows of huge white teeth.

The stallion was a handsome, but gigantic, black and white paint. He stepped closer to Novana, and caressed her sweating neck with his muzzle. He then began to lick her face. Novana's eyes had no fear, only despair.

Fury was filled with a deep rage. He reared, screaming as loud as a barn full of horses, and ran toward the other stallion. The paint was taken by surprise. He immediately tried to untangle his long legs to fight back, but Fury was in such a rage he might as well have been fighting a demon.

Soon Fury had the paint thrown off his feet, and a violent battle ensued. When Fury finally stopped fighting, the paint scrambled to his feet, and whistled. Five large young stallions trotted up.

"Hold him!" the paint yelled out the order. The young horses threw Fury down, and stood over him so he couldn't get up.

"You will see what happens to horses that interfere with my herd!" Fury was roughly pushed to his feet. The paint stallion came over and stood two feet away from Fury's face.

"Who are you and what are you doing here?" the big horse growled.

Fury glared down at the paint's feet. The paint stallion's mares gasped. The stallion's eyes narrowed with hate.

"Answer me," he hissed. Fury refused to answer.

"I know who he is!" One of the young stallions cried. Fury looked to see who it was, and didn't believe his eyes. It was Samson, the colt he had beaten months ago! The sorrel horse's eyes were gleaming with anticipation. The paint nodded.

"Go on…"

Samson grinned. "That," he said, "is Fury, son of *Sariavo!*" The paint smiled, and the smile was very evil.

"Well, we might as well get rid of him, so we will show Sariavo that his offspring can be killed." The stallions cheered.

Samson's grin faded. "You mean to *kill* him?"

The paint nodded gleefully. "He is going to Death Mountain!"

~ 10 ~

Death Mountain

Samson's grin had disappeared fully. "But…he…" The paint shook his head.

"No. He is far too dangerous." The stallion turned to Fury.

"I am Durango. You are foolish to come here. You will die on top of Death Mountain for doing so."

Fury had heard tales of Death Mountain. It was a 2,000-foot drop off. At the bottom of the overhanging cliff, thousands of sharp rocks decorated the floor. Fury's eyes darkened slightly. Durango laughed.

"Yes, even the most powerful and brave stallion fears the drop off."

Novana screamed. "No! I cannot bear to live if he dies!" Diamond rushed to the hysterical mare and tried to sooth her.

Fury fought his captors furiously. Durango laughed even harder.

"Just think, in the future, she will have my foals." His smile was so evil it could have frozen the sun itself. Fury bellowed fiercely.

"Well, let's get this over with. Bring him along." Durango, Samson, and another stallion named Apache led Fury away towards his fearful fate. Novana screamed again, then fainted.

Fury concentrated on the path in front of him. His tail didn't arch proudly like it usually did, but drooped, dragging itself along behind him. He knew that escape was not possible. The other three stallions were just as big and powerful as he was. He thought about Novana, who had been his lifelong companion.

She would now be subject to Durango, to satisfy his every whim and fancy. He thought about Glory, his son. The white colt would not be able to understand that his 'hero' was dead.

Then Fury's thoughts turned to his father. Sariavo was a strong stallion. He wouldn't say much. He would just want to be alone. Fury wondered what it would be like, falling 2,000 feet down.

Fury's thoughts were interrupted suddenly. "Here we are. Bring him here! Hurry up, Apache, we don't have all day!" Durango growled.

Fury felt himself being pushed forwards. He looked ahead. Two feet of trail remained, then nothing. Fury struggled violently, only to be struck heavily on the head by a hoof.

His head now hung over the cliff. Fury looked at the rocks. They seemed so close, so…deathly. Durango walked over and stood next to Fury.

"Well, any last things you want us to know?" Fury stared at the pinto stallion, which was sneering at him.

"No? Well, then push him over!" Durango stepped back.

******

Suddenly, Fury stopped inching forward. He heard angry grunts and squeals of fighting stallions behind him. He expected a hoof to knock him head over heels down the cliff. But nothing came.

Fury turned his head around and focused his uncooperative eyes on the scene behind him. Samson had kicked Apache, who had then run back down the mountain in fright, and now was fighting with Durango.

Durango stood, lowered his head, and rammed Samson, right in the chest, forcing the sorrel stallion to back towards the cliff edge. Samson tried to go forward, but Durango stood firm.

After a great effort, Samson was able to work himself around so that he was away from the edge.

He dug his hooves into the rock and pushed forward, so that Durango now struggled at the edge. Fury stepped in.

"Samson, let him go."

Silence fell. Samson turned to Fury, his eyes wide with surprise.

"What? Let him go?" Samson asked, incredulously. Fury nodded, and looked at Durango.

"I'm going to let you go, because I don't believe that killing you will solve anything. My herd is mine, and I will take yours as well, but I will not kill you."

Durango's shocked eyes shifted from one stallion to the other. Then, finally, he nodded.

"I will go," Durango snarled.

Fury motioned towards the path. Durango trotted down the path, still breathing heavily from his ordeal. Fury turned to Samson. The younger stallion was still staring at him.

"I can't believe you did that!" Samson said.

Fury frowned. "Though I may someday regret my decision, it is better to change your enemies into friends. And it is my hope that he learned from this experience."

Samson sighed. "Now that you explain it, it does make sense."

Fury looked closely at Samson. "Why did you save me?" he asked.

Samson lowered his head. "I couldn't believe it when you beat me. You…kinda were my hero, I guess. I didn't want Durango to kill you."

Fury grinned. "Well, I for one am sure glad he didn't!" Samson chuckled.

"Something else, too," Samson said. "Your dad was Sariavo, and he sounded familiar to me, so I asked my dad who he was. My dad is Lightning, your dad's brother." Fury stared at Samson.

"That means that you are my cousin?" Samson nodded.

Fury grinned again. The two stallions stood there for a minute. Then, Fury started back along the trail towards the herd. Samson followed silently.

****

When they came into sight of the herd, Novana spotted them. Her mouth dropped, and her entire body relaxed. She gave a small cry and rushed forward. Fury ran towards her, and the two stopped about a foot away from each other. Fury looked into Novana's eyes.

"Somehow I knew I was going to see you again," the black mare said softly. Fury chuckled.

"Am I that predictable?"

Novana laughed.

******

That night, Fury was startled from sleep by a strange noise. It sounded like a cough, but softer. He started towards the sound, being cautious. The noise stopped.

"Hello?" Fury called quietly into the trees.

"Please, I don't mean any harm, please, don't hurt me…"the voice turned to sobs. Fury could tell by the tone of the voice that it was either a filly or a young mare. He immediately softened his own voice.

"It's alright; I promise I won't hurt you. Come out." A shadow came from the trees. Fury almost gasped when he saw it. It was a young mare, dappled gray, but she had big cuts all over her legs and shoulders. A big bruise decorated the right side of her face. She looked at the ground, lowering her head. Silent sobs shook her small body.

~ 11 ~

Daydream

"What's your name?" Fury asked her gently. The beautifully shaped head came up a little.

"Daydream, but my owner called me Dream." Fury stared at her.

"Your *owner*? You mean a human?" he asked, incredulously. She nodded.

"They aren't so bad, but my owner gave me to his son for a wedding gift. The son's name was Henry, and he was mean to me. So one day, I tried to run away. But I got stuck in a barbed wire fence. That was yesterday, I think," she paused, thinking.

"I finally freed myself this morning, and, here I am. I was just wandering, and I wanted to sleep close to a herd of wild horses, just in case something happened during the night. I'm sorry I disturbed you. I'll leave now." She started back into the forest.

Fury stepped in front of her. "You don't have to leave. You can stay with my herd if you like."

Dream looked up at him from underneath long eyelashes. Fury felt like his heart was melting. She reminded him of his mother. She had obviously been through a great deal and he wanted to help.

"You could sleep by my herd, if you want to."

She smiled. "Oh, that would be wonderful, if you're sure its no problem." Fury shook his head. The two started back towards the herd.

******

When Novana woke up the next morning, she started. A small dappled gray mare was sleeping next to Fury. She flattened her ears, and started towards the sleeping duo. Fury's eyes opened slightly, then widened when he saw Novana glaring at him.

"What do you think you're doing?" Novana asked in a strained voice. Fury was wide-awake, but Novana's sharp words woke up Dream.

She opened her eyes quickly, and stared at the ground, trembling, when Novana glared at her. Fury stepped between Novana and Dream.

"Novana, it's okay. I found her last night, over in the woods. She escaped from humans. I let her sleep by us so she could have safe place to rest." Novana's look changed from anger to pity.

"Oh, you poor thing, you're covered in cuts. Let's go to the stream and get you cleaned up." Dream smiled shakily and followed Novana to the stream of water that flowed through the clearing. Fury followed the two mares, watching Novana's tail swishing from side to side while she moved. He sighed. She really was beautiful. Gorgeous. Glorious. Amazing. Smart. Special.

Fury stopped himself. Shaking his head, he watched as Novana gently washed the cuts on Dream's slim legs. Then, she started to clean a deep cut on Dream's shoulder. Dream gasped, then wiggled away. Novana looked up at her.

"I'm sorry. I'll try to be gentler." Fury chuckled, wondering if Novana could be any gentler than she already was. Again Novana touched water to the cut. Fury saw Dream bite her lip, and grimace.

"There, much better," Novana said when she was all done. Fury turned to go back to the clearing, and almost ran smack into Samson.

The younger stallion grinned, sheepishly. "She is pretty, isn't she?" Samson said in a whisper. Fury laughed.

"Yep. She would be a good match for you, but you need to bring her out of her shyness first." Samson's smile could've melted ice.

"You think I could?"

Fury nodded. "Sure. But you're going to need a lot of flowers," he teased. Samson chuckled, then walked over to Dream.

"Hey, uh… you want to…um…maybe if you aren't busy…uh…If I could…you might…" Dream's eyes were full of laughter, but she looked up at Samson seriously.

"If I could what?" she asked sweetly. Fury barely kept from laughing out loud. Samson turned redder than his already red coat.

"Um, want to go to the...waterfall? There are a lot of water lilies, and if you wanted one, you could maybe braid it into your tail. That would be pretty," Samson finished.

Dream smiled, and Fury could see that Samson was totally enchanted by the young mare. Fury glanced at Novana, who stared at him, and then her eyes rolled. Fury almost laughed, but started instead to cough. Dream started off in the direction of the waterfall. Samson immediately followed.

"Do you like grass seeds? I love grass seeds. They have a really good after taste! But I absolutely love wild onions, don't you?" Dream looked over her shoulder at him.

"Oh, yes, I..." But Samson had gone to another subject. "I think moose are strange. Why on earth would they shed their antlers? Now, if I were a moose..." His voice trailed off.

Novana looked at Fury, who looked back at her, and they started to laugh as hard as they could. Soon they were crying, they were laughing so hard.

Finally, when the laughter subsided, Fury smiled at his mare. "You are beautiful, you know that?"

Novana's forelock fell over her eyes, and Fury brushed it off with his nose. Novana smiled back at him.

"Well, you are very special, Fury. I love you." Fury grinned. This had the makings of a great day.

~ 12 ~

A New Life

That evening, Fury noticed that Dream and Samson were off in a shadowy corner of the clearing, away from the other horses. They were talking, and suddenly, Dream squealed and put her forehead to Samson's chest. Fury wondered if Samson had asked her to be his mate.

But then Dream said, "Oh, Samson! That was a funny joke. You are so good at telling jokes!" Fury sighed. Those two were such a good pair. Samson whispered something to Dream, and then came over to Fury.

"I was wondering if you think I should ask her to be my…mate?" Fury chuckled, deep in his throat.

"That is your decision, and I can't make it for you. But, she is a great choice for you." Samson looked nervous. Fury decided not to ask if he was, and so embarrass him. Samson took a deep breath, and then looked up.

"I'm going to do it!" Then he started back towards Dream. A moment later, Fury heard Samson say, "But, Dream…you…"

"Samson, I'm just not sure if I'm ready. I want to be sure." Dream stated, looking uncomfortable. Samson's head drooped.

"I want you to be my mate so horribly, Dream. I love you." Dream smiled through her tears.

"I know you do, Samson. I love you to. I'm not saying no. I just want to get some advice on this. I'll talk to Novana." After saying that, Dream ran toward Novana, tears running down her face.

Fury looked back at Samson. The sorrel stallion was standing in the same spot, shaking with sorrow. He looked at Fury, and the moonlight revealed a lone tear on his cheek. He walked dejectedly toward Fury. He looked Fury full in the face.

"You are more like a big brother to me. What should I do?" he asked. Fury looked the young male straight in the eyes.

"You are a stallion, Samson. *Stallions do not cry.*" Samson gulped, and wiped the tear away on a front leg.

"Sorry, Fury. But that really hurt." Fury nodded. "I know. But she didn't say no, did she?" Samson shook his head.

Fury continued, "Okay. So she still might say yes. So don't act like she refused you. Look. I felt the same way once. Novana refused me straight out the first time I asked her to be a part of my herd. I thought that my life was over. I hated myself, thinking I wasn't perfect enough for her."

Fury paused. His face was full of memories.

"Then I realized something. I found that I had to be patient. So, I waited. I got to know Novana better. Then, I asked her again. Obviously, you can see that the second time went much better!" Samson nodded.

"So, if I'm not supposed to marry Dream, our Creator will let me know, somehow?" Fury nodded.

"The Creator will always give you an answer. It might not be what you wanted it to be, but it is always for the best."

Samson grinned. "So, should I ask her again?"

Fury looked seriously at the younger stallion. "Yes. Not tonight, but soon."

******

The following morning, Fury and the herd members could feel the tension between Samson and Dream. The herd waited quietly.

After lunch, Samson approached Dream. "We need to talk."

She shook her head, her eyes sparkling. "No, Samson, we don't. I accept your offer, if you still want me."

Samson laughed. The two stood there for a minute, looking at each other. Then Samson inched his nose forward. Soon, it met Dream's.

The herd burst into bedlam. The horses neighed their approval. Novana stood, a tear shining in her eye. "Congratulations."

Dream smiled. "Thank you. Thank you very, very much."

~ 13 ~

The Journey Home

The next few days passed in a blur of activity. The herd worked a full day to make the clearing decorative for a small celebration for Samson and Dream.

The two geldings, Jake and Runner, helped put up a rock arch, from larger rocks rolled up from the stream. Then the mares threw grape vines over the arch to make it more festive.

There was a pile of food in the middle of the clearing. There were grapes, grass seeds, wild onions, and some wild wheat corn that was found in an abandoned farm field.

Samson and Dream had no idea that this was going on, because they had gone to the waterfall for the day, to swim and talk about the future. They returned just before supper.

Dream entered the clearing first, and she gasped when she saw all the decorations and the food. Samson stepped out beside her and his mouth fell open.

"Surprise!" the herd yelled at them. Fury stepped forward.

"A little something to celebrate the beginning of your new herd." Dream recovered her voice.

"Thank you all so very much. This is amazing!" Soon, all the horses were crowding around the food, laughing and talking to the new couple. Fury stayed a little distance away from everybody else. Suddenly, he got an idea. He walked over to Novana, and whispered in her ear. She smiled and nodded.

"Okay everyone!" she called. "After you are done eating, we are going to have games!" The herd cheered.

Soon, the herd had been divided into two teams. Fury led one, and Samson led the other. A spirited game of Capture the Lead Mare began. Novana was voted the Lead Mare of Fury's group, so she went off and hid. Samson chose Daydream as his lead mare. After playing for three hours, Fury's group finally found Dream and won. The herd slowly made its way back to the clearing, laughing about their blunders during the game.

Novana found Fury at the food pile, and nudged him with her muzzle. He looked down at her.

"What is it, Novana?"

She smiled sadly, and cocked her head towards Inahu. Fury followed her gaze and saw his daughter walking through the trees with a young gray stallion. They were deep in a conversation, their ears pricked to catch every little word the other said.

Fury realized with a start that his daughter had grown up so much during the last few weeks. She was even more beautiful than she had been as a filly.

"Our daughter won't be with us much longer, Fury. All the young stallions are in love with her already, and she's barely over a year old."

Both Fury and Novana walked over to the circle of horses that were talking.

Diamond looked at her, and said, "Novana! Do that beautiful dance that your mother taught you!"

The herd bellowed its agreement. Novana laughed, and stood inside the circle that the herd members formed. She began to lift her feet over each other, performing a flawless "passage", a movement that was part of her Spanish dancing horse heritage from her mother's bloodline. The herd watched, enchanted, as Novana tossed her head gracefully from side to side, her legs barely touching the ground before they were snapped up again.

When she finally stopped, all the horses were silently breathless at Novana's beautiful dance. Fury whistled at her, and then began to lift his feet in a trotting movement. With a laugh, Novana started to trot in place, too, and then they went faster. Fury grinned. This was great fun! Faster and faster they trotted, never moving from the spot they'd started in until Fury thought if they went still faster, his legs might fall off.

Suddenly, they stopped. Fury faced Novana again, breathless. Then, the herd started to cheer as loud as they could. Novana stood next to Fury, and the two bowed. It was a great ending to an unforgettable night.

****

After the excitement of Samson and Daydream's special day was over, Fury talked to Novana about going back to his father's herd, or close to it.

"Novana, I feel like going home now. I love this place, but it isn't the same." Novana nodded.

"I know. I want to go home too." So go home they did. The herd separated into three groups. The original herd, Fury's group, headed for Sariavo's area.

Fury gave Durango's old herd of shaggy mares to a young stallion named Copper, and they went into the forested hills.

Samson and Daydream bade their friends a tearful goodbye, and disappeared, heading west to find more herd members for their new herd.

******

About three hours away from the home cave, Fury stopped. The horses wanted to finish the journey, but he could tell that they were exhausted.

"We'll sleep here," he told them. "Then, we'll go the rest of the way tomorrow morning." The herd bedded down, some lying on their sides, others sleeping in the normal way, standing up. Novana slowly lowered herself to the ground, grunting softly when she hit. Fury smiled. It was a sure sign that his mare was carrying a foal. He walked over to her.

"Am I right in assuming that I am going to be a sire to another foal soon?" he asked quietly. She looked up at him, and nodded.

"Yes. Are you sure you wanted a third?" she asked. Fury grinned.

"I honestly don't care how many we have. As long as they are healthy." Novana laughed.

"Easy for you to say. You don't have to do all the work." Fury chuckled.

"Sure. We stallions don't do anything. We just fight predators, drive off other stallions, and starve so our mares can have what little there is…" Novana tossed her head in exasperation.

"Enough. I get the picture," she laughed.

******

Fury woke the herd early. He wanted to get a good head start. Inahu was getting too big to ride on Fury's back, so she stumbled along, her eyes half closed. Fury looked back at her and grinned.

"You awake, Princess?" he used his most favored nickname for her. She opened one eye.

"No, I don't think so, Dad. I'm so tired…" the eye closed again. Fury chuckled.

They came to the hill that overlooked the big cave that was Fury's home. He sighed. It was good to be back.

"Hello, everybody! We're back!" Four horses came to the cave entrance: Sariavo, Penny, Sari and Glory, who stood proudly by his grandfather. A grin lit Sariavo's face.

"Hello, to all!" he called up. Fury raced down the hill, planted a kiss on his mother's cheek, and bowed slightly to his father. "Hello, Father." Sariavo gave a hearty laugh.

"Come in, come in, I think the pool would be a remedy to prescribe for all of you."

Fury smiled. "That does sound good."

All the horses soon found their way to the acre large swimming pool inside the cave. The cave was larger than a small village, so there was plenty of room for the whole herd.

Sari and Penny fell in love with Inahu, and gave her a special room, that they had made for her, with a bed of soft grass, a small pool the size of a bathroom, and a little pile of roses on the floor. Inahu loved it.

"Oh, it's beautiful!" she said, and popped into the water.

"It's warm! The water is so warm, it feels so good!" She sighed.

"Thank you, Grandma and Grams." Sari was Grandma, and Penny was Grams. Sariavo was Poppa to the grand foals.

Sariavo came over to the big pool where Fury was busy swimming. The older stallion slipped into the pool.

Sariavo smiled at his stepson. "I heard from a little bird that you and Novana will be parents to three soon."

Fury nodded. "Yes, we will."

Sariavo asked, "Do you plan to stay here, or are you going to find a place close by?"

Fury thought for a minute. "I think, if it isn't a problem for you, I will stay here, for the time being."

Sariavo nodded. "That would be fine, if you're sure that's what you want."

Fury nodded. "I want to stay at home."

~ 14 ~

Home of the Brave

A few days after his return, Fury started to notice a difference in his father's attitude. He wasn't cheerful anymore, but sad and dejected.

Several times Sariavo went to visit his parents. One day, he came home, dragging his feet and lowering his head. Glory, who was now a yearling, ran up to him.

"Grandpa, what's wrong?" Sariavo glared at him.

"I'm fine, Glory," he growled. Then he disappeared into the cave.

Glory's head fell, and his tail drooped sadly. Fury walked over to his son. The white colt was shaking, and a tear ran down his face, followed by another. Fury narrowed his eyes.

"Glory, if you want to be a true stallion, you have to learn not to cry," Fury said gravely. Glory looked up, hiccupped, and wiped his eyes on a foreleg.

"Thanks Dad." Fury's face softened.

"That's okay. I know that what Grandpa said hurt you. I'll go talk to him." With that, Fury trotted into the cave, and to his father's room.

He kicked at the stone entrance, "Sariavo? It's Fury. Can I come in?"

Receiving no answer, he stepped into the dimly lit room. His father lay on his grass bed, staring at the wall.

"I'm not going anywhere." Fury grinned.

"I know. I'm not stupid enough to try to move you." He heard a soft chuckle.

"What's up? Do you want to talk about it?" Fury asked. Sariavo rolled over, and stood up. His magnificent body was still at least a half a foot taller than his son's.

"My mother died today," he said simply. Fury's face fell.

"I'm sorry. Casablanca was a fine mare." Sariavo's eyes hardened so they seemed like stone. "She was NOT just a fine mare, Fury! How can you talk that way?"

Fury nodded. "I didn't mean it to sound like that." The conversation was interrupted by the sound of a scream. Fury jerked around.

"That's Novana!" he said, and whirled out of the cave, Sariavo was right behind him.

Fury took in the scene before him. A pack of at least thirty wolves were chasing after the herd members.

Two wolves had Sari backed into a corner. They were slashing at her delicate legs. She was fighting back, but she wasn't strong enough.

With a start of surprise, the seriousness of the wolf attack sank into Fury's mind. He saw his father standing beside him.

Sariavo looked at Fury, and Fury looked at his father.

"Let's put this pack in the ground," Sariavo said, his voice filled with anger and hate.

"Dad, if I die, it will be an honor to die beside you," Fury quoted the famous words. Sariavo nodded. "Let's go!"

Jake and Runner stood beside them, and soon Glory had the other young stallions rounded up. A few of the mares were trapped, but a lot of them managed to get out of the situations they were in and run behind the males and into the cave. Sari and Novana were the only two that were seriously in danger. The stallions and geldings formed a line in front of the cave.

Sariavo bellowed, and the sound sent chills into the bodies of the wolves. There were eleven stallions, and two geldings, against thirty-three wolves.

Fury followed suit and bellowed, just as loud as his father had. All the other males raised their voices as well, and the air echoed and reechoed the anger in their voices.

Sariavo lowered his head, and charged. All the males followed. Fury headed straight for Novana, who was surrounded by three wolves; drool dripping from their fangs. She was scared, but was furiously kicking at her tormentors. One of the wolves ventured to close, and he was snapped back by one of her flying hind feet. Fury charged right into the middle of the other two, and soon the wolves had been driven away.

Fury shouted above the noise, "Novana, get into the cave, NOW!"

She obeyed quickly. Fury then turned his attention to his son. The white colt had been taken down, and only his thrashing hooves kept the canines away. Fury raced to his son's rescue, his flashing teeth getting a few yelps and howls in return for their work.

Soon, Glory was on his feet and making quick work of another wolf. Fury went to help his father, who was struggling to free Sari from five of the furry predators.

The fight lasted only fifteen minutes. Thirty-two wolves were dead, only one had escaped.

Four young stallions were dead, and a huge brute wolf, undoubtedly the leader, had killed the sorrel gelding, Runner. Jake was wounded slightly, with a gash on his hock. Fury looked for Glory, and saw him helping one of the young horses clean a bite on his leg.

Fury searched for Sariavo, but didn't see him anywhere. He caught sight of his father, helping Sari get up.

Suddenly, Fury was thrown off his feet by a big black body. It was Novana.

She licked his face furiously, murmuring, "You're alive, you're alive," over and over. Fury heard laughter behind him. His father was laughing at him.

"Having some trouble with your wife there, Fury?" Fury made a face at him, and then gently pushed Novana aside.

"Yes I'm alive, yes I'm wounded, and no, it's not serious."

Novana sighed. "I'm so thankful you aren't hurt badly." Fury slowly walked over to his father, who smiled at him. Fury then was aware of another presence. His son, Glory, was standing next to him. Sariavo beamed at them.

"You both are fine stallions. You fought bravely." Glory straightened.

"Thank you, Grandpa. I see you haven't lost any of your strength. You are still as glorious as you ever were." Sariavo chuckled.

"Maybe not. Your father and I have written our legends. Our days of glory and honor are pretty much over. But you are here to take our place. It's your turn to write a legend of your own." Glory thought for a minute.

"I only hope it's one that mothers will tell their foals for years to come."

Epilogue

Novana gave birth to a daughter three months later, and Fury named her Sequoia (pronounced Secoya). Sariavo's father, Regal, died four weeks later, and Sariavo was heartbroken. But, as he told Glory, the colt had to write his own legend in the hearts of all wild horses. And, no doubt, he would.

About The Author...

Victoria Kasten was born in 1991. She has loved horses since she could walk. She began taking English riding lessons at age nine, and continued with the lessons until age thirteen.

She has two horses, a mischievous Quarter Horse/Pony of America gelding named Looky, and a beautiful registered bay Quarter Horse mare named Katie.

She discovered her love of writing at age ten, when she wrote a short story called The Wild Mustang. She also began to write poems, two of which were published in a national Christian newspaper.

Her first Mighty Stallion book was begun in 2002, at age eleven; and finished the year after, at age twelve.

Victoria hopes to be able to be a full time author after she finishes college. She enjoys many hobbies such as researching Medieval History; spending time outside on her family's farm with her cats, rabbits, horses and alpacas; and having squirt gun fights with her parents.

Already in Print!

Mighty Stallion

Join Fury's father, Sariavo, the mighty stallion, as he embarks on the grand adventure that started it all.

Mighty Stallion 3 Glory's Legend

This is the exciting story of Fury's son Glory. Travel with him to an Indian tribe, where he befriends the chief, and discovers the meaning of true friendship

Mighty Stallion 4 Dancer's Dream

Another adventure is coming your way! Dancer, Fury's granddaughter, along with her two friends Titan and Lily, embarks on an adventure that includes a raging snowstorm, captivity by a wagon train, and finding friendship in unlikely places…

Sneak Peek!
Mighty Stallion 3
Glory's Legend!

Just as the sun peeked over the canyon, a group of bronze skinned riders appeared in the bottom of the canyon, riding spotted horses. They whispered excitedly as they saw the six good-looking mares and the prized albino stallion. They pulled their ropes out of leather saddlebags stolen from white settlers, and moved silently forward.

Glory couldn't smell them, because the wind was moving away from him towards the Indians. He slept unaware of the coming danger.

When the Indians reached the herd, not one of the horses was awake. At the first sound of the whooping humans, they jumped up and fled towards the trail leading out of the canyon.

A young gray mare stumbled and fell, and was quickly captured by one of the braves. The other six horses sped on, trying their utmost to stay ahead of their pursuers.

Glory saw a rope settle around Grace's neck, pulling her to a stop. Finally, all the mares were gone, leaving Glory to flee alone. A muscular warrior galloped after Glory, his rope coiled and ready.

Glory whirled sharply and ran into a small, box canyon. In an instant, he saw his mistake. Three walls surrounded him. The trail was a dead end. He turned to see the Indian ride slowly into the canyon, his rope held high. Glory screamed angrily, not wanting to be a prisoner.

The rope flew over Glory's neck. The young stallion bucked and reared, fighting the warrior. The Indian held on to the rope, letting the albino wear himself out.

Once Glory saw there was no escape, he stopped fighting the rope, and glared furiously at the human who held him captive. The man began to lead Glory back to the village, and Glory vowed to get his mares and himself free as soon as possible.

Write To The Author!!!

Victoria would love to hear from you! You can write a letter to her at:

Mighty Stallion Books
5465 Glencoe Ave
Webster, MN 55088

She would also like to hear your suggestions and opinions on her writing. If you fill out the form on the following page and send it to her, she can get a better idea of how to serve her fans.

Name

_____

Age (optional) _____

Have you enjoyed the Mighty Stallion Books so far?

_____

What have you liked most about them?

_____

_____

_____

Who is your favorite character, and why?

_____

_____

_____

What type of book would you like to see Victoria write?

_____

What didn't you like about the Mighty Stallion books so far?

_____

_____

Your Address:

_____

_____

Mighty Stallion Mail Order Form
Use this convenient order form to order additional copies!

PLEASE PRINT:

NAME: _____

ADDRESS: _____

CITY: _____   STATE: _____

ZIP: _____   PHONE: _____

_____ Copies Mighty Stallion 1 @ $8.95 each $_____

_____ Copies Mighty Stallion 2 Fury's $_____
      Journey @ $8.95 each

_____ Copies Mighty Stallion 3 Glory's Legend $_____
      @ $8.95 each

_____ Copies Mighty Stallion 4 Dancer's Dream $_____
      @ $8.95 each

Postage & handling @ $2 per book/$1 for $_____
      each additional book

Minnesota Residents Please add 6.5% Sales Tax $_____

Total Amount Enclosed: $_____

Make Checks payable to: Victoria Kasten

Send To: Mighty Stallion Books, 5465 Glencoe Ave, Webster, MN
55088